D0575678

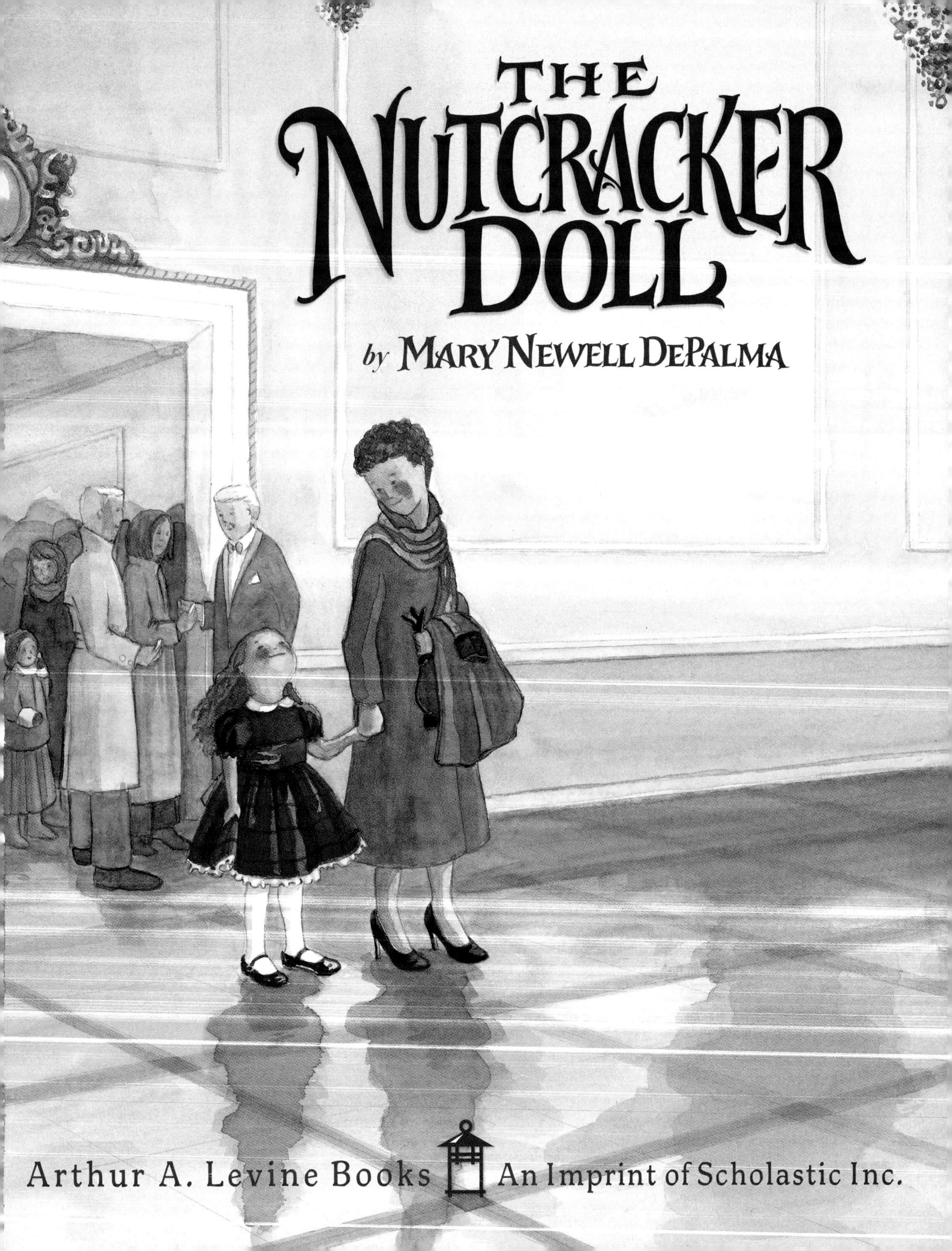

The Nutcracker Doll

by Mary Newell DePalma

Arthur A. Levine Books · An Imprint of Scholastic Inc.

Library of Congress Cataloging-in-Publication Data
DePalma, Mary Newell.
The Nutcracker doll / by Mary Newell DePalma. -- 1st ed.
p. cm.
Summary: Kepley, a young ballerina, gets to play a flower doll in a professional production of "The Nutcracker."
ISBN-10: 0-439-80242-3 / ISBN-13: 978-0-439-80242-0
[1. Ballet--Fiction.] I. Title. PZ7.D4385Nut 2006 [E]--dc22
2006016466

10 9 8 7 6 5 4 3 2 1 07 08 09 10 11

The art for this book was created using watercolor and pen and ink.
Book design by Elizabeth Parisi
First edition, October 2007 • Printed in Singapore 46

For Kepley, with love.

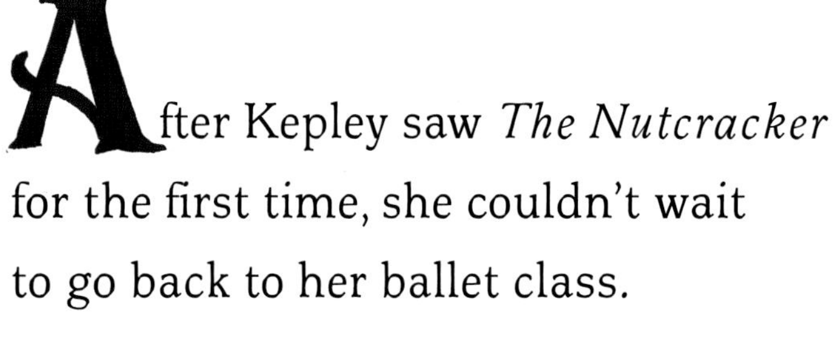

After Kepley saw *The Nutcracker* for the first time, she couldn't wait to go back to her ballet class.

Kepley recognized two of the older girls dressing for their class. "I saw you in *The Nutcracker*," Kepley said shyly. "You were great!"

"Next year you should try out!" they said. "It's so much fun."

From then on, Kepley paid extra special attention in her ballet class.
She wanted to dance beautifully in *The Nutcracker.*

304
205
215
BALLET
218

One sunny Saturday,
the ballet building was filled with excited girls,
all bouncing, fidgeting, and giggling.
It was Nutcracker audition day.

The girls grew quiet and still
as they lined up for their audition.
Kepley straightened her number: 215.
Her insides felt funny.
She didn't know what would happen next.

217
215

When it was her turn, Kepley's heart was thumping.
She remembered to smile, and did her best.

215

It was a whole week before the letter from the ballet finally arrived.

"Congratulations!" it began.
Kepley jumped up and down with excitement. She was a doll!

They practiced every Saturday, but Kepley didn't dance much.

"What do you mean you just stand still?" asked Mom.

"I'm supposed to be a doll standing
under the Christmas tree," explained Kepley,
"so I can't move. Then I'm carried offstage by a giant mouse!"

"You can't move," said Mom. "Suppose you have to sneeze?"

Kepley hadn't thought about that.
Sneezing didn't turn out to be a problem,

but giggling was.
The girls couldn't stop giggling
during rehearsal at the theatre.
After all, it *was* silly to be carried offstage
by a man pretending to be a giant mouse!

As they neared the performance date,
Kepley was measured,
fitted, and photographed.

LLET

Finally, the girls were ready.

Kepley felt very important
and professional
the day of the first performance.

She had a backstage pass
and could enter the theatre
through the stage door.

She listened to the music and
stage directions on the intercom
and knew when it was time
to get dressed.

All of the dolls felt like princesses in their costumes.
It was time to go backstage.

It was very dark in the wings.
The brightly lit stage
looked like a different world.

When Kepley heard her cue,
she took a deep breath and
stepped into the warm lights.

The lights were blinding.
Kepley could feel the music in her chest,
and the stage shook underfoot.

Suddenly, everything turned sideways
as the mouse whisked her offstage!

"Good job!"
whispered the mouse,
and that was it!
It happened so quickly.
Kepley couldn't wait to do it again.

Kepley was in a dozen performances
of *The Nutcracker*,
each one as exciting as the first.
She loved the cocoon of the wings,
the costumes, and the lights.

Someday maybe she could dance
the Waltz of the Flowers,

but for now, being a doll was a dream come true.